Jöns Mellgren

Elsa and the Night

LITTLE
GESTALTEN

Elsa is sitting by the kitchen table, sorting through her granola. "Number seventy-eight," she mumbles, picking out another raisin. All the lamps are burning. It's warm in the room.

Outside, it's getting light. She sips her coffee. It's bitter.
A scratching sound can be heard from underneath the sofa.
Elsa bends down and shines the light of her hurricane lamp.
Something dark is moving under there.

Elsa puts down a saucer with sugar cubes on it.
When the creature is brave enough to come out
and have a taste, she grabs it and holds it up to
the light. It cries out and wriggles like a fish.

She puts it down next to the cereal box.
Now she sees what it is—and it's neither an animal
nor a ghost. It's the Night that's found its way into
her home. It's trembling like a sewing machine and
lets out small, cold puffs of breath.

"You're not allowed to be here," says Elsa.
She puts the Night into an old cake tin, pouring
some of the raisins in too. Then she goes down to
the boiler room in the basement. She puts the tin
in a corner, behind the boiler. Then she hurries
out and slams the steel door shut.

She goes and sits on her balcony. The sun is shining over the city. Fourteen hours later, it's still just as light. People on the streets are yawning and rubbing their eyes.
"That's the way the cookie crumbles," mutters Elsa. "It's not my fault."

Time passes. The birds get hoarse and stop singing. Owls and bats fly drowsily through the streets. But it doesn't get dark.

Elsa sighs deeply. Then she goes down to the boiler room again and fetches the Night. She pulls down the blinds before she opens the tin. The Night has shrunk and gone a bit pale around the edges, but at least it has eaten some of the raisins.

Elsa pours a glass of blackberry juice. The Night
drinks it all in one gulp.
"Have you seen this old tub?" says Elsa, turning the
ship in a bottle. "Her name is *Ottelina*. I worked in
the kitchen when I was young."

"We traveled the globe, but I mostly sat in the galley, peeling potatoes. Sometimes we transported wild animals. Then I fed them with potato peelings."

"Then, one stormy night, we ran aground. The ship split in two. In the glare of a flash of lightning, I saw an elephant bobbing up and down among the waves. I clung on tightly to his back."

"The next morning, we drifted ashore an island. I named the elephant Olaf. It was a simple life: we fished and looked after the lighthouse. Occasionally, tourists came by. We practiced a circus trick, which we performed for them."

Elsa clears her throat and looks out the window.
Then she picks up her handkerchief and dries
her eyes. Gently, the Night puts a hand on hers.

And Elsa tells the Night what happened:
That Olaf got sick and no medicines could help.
She moved up into the lighthouse.
Night after night, year after year, she sat awake in the light of the gas lamp.

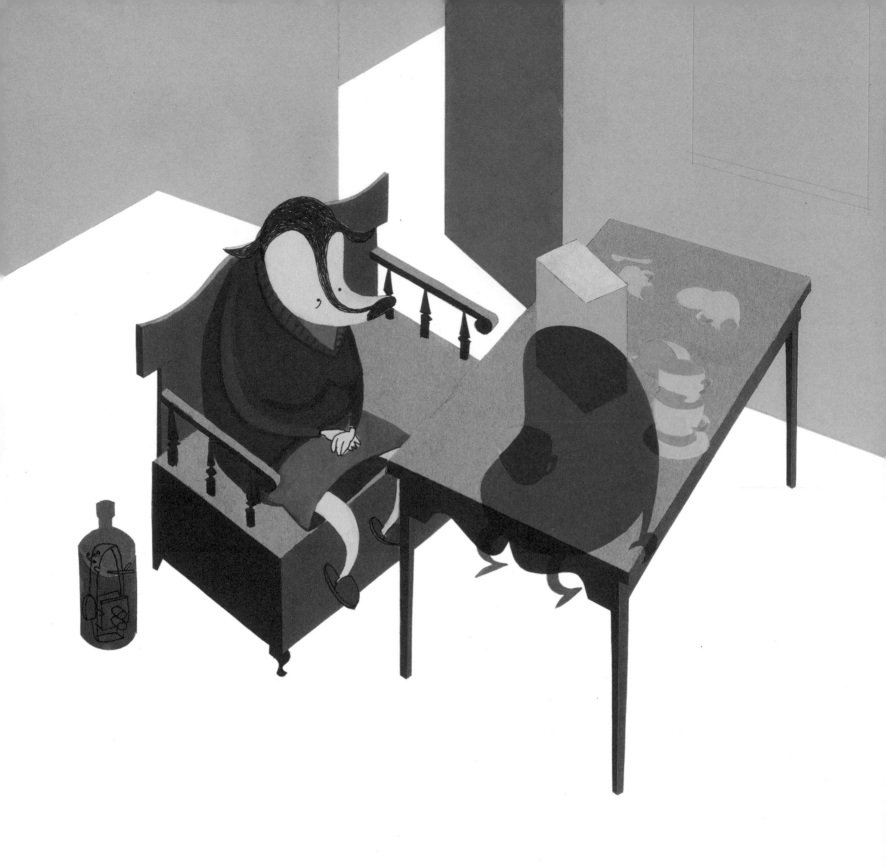

"The lighthouse works on electricity now and nobody needs to guard it anymore. But I got used to having it light. I haven't slept a wink for thirty years."

Elsa sits quietly for a while. Then she goes out into the hallway. She buttons up her coat and laces up her boots. "You look better now," she says to the Night. "But take the umbrella to avoid the sun."

The asphalt on the roads has softened in the hot sunshine. People are squinting up at the sky. They are dazzled by the light and have gotten dizzy and quarrelsome for lack of sleep. There are crashed cars everywhere. Everyone they meet has big bags under their eyes.

"Would you like some candy?" asks Elsa.
The Night points to a box of licorice fish.
"We'll go to the flower shop afterwards," says
Elsa. "We're going to buy lilies of the valley."

"This is where Olaf is buried, under this oak tree," says Elsa. "I rowed ashore with the skeleton myself." The Night devours the last licorice fish. A tear runs down Elsa's cheek. It falls on the ground without a sound.

"I remember how we used to swim out to sea,"
says Elsa, and yawns. "Early in the morning
before the fog had lifted. It was beautiful."
The Night strokes her hair. Then it carefully
lifts her up in its arms.

The Night walks through the city now, moving more silently than a cat. It picks up the candy man and the children playing by the fountain.

Then it takes the fishmongers and the whole marching band. Everyone the Night meets, it lifts up and carries with it. And it grows bigger and bigger.

It walks with huge, swaying steps and breathes cool winds over the city.

Then the Night hums a song about the moonlight and warm slippers. It empties the streets and puts an end to all the quarrels. It goes from house to house, tucking everyone into bed.

Last of all, it lays a cover over Elsa.
She's already fast asleep … and
dreaming.

Jöns Mellgren (born 1976) is a Swedish author, filmmaker, and illustrator. His first children's picture book, *Jungle Night,* was published in 1999 and was followed by *Mustafa and the Storm* in 2009 and *Rufus in the Underworld* in 2010. The radio play of *Mustafa and the Storm* was nominated for Sweden's public media service award, *Ikarospriset,* in the category of best drama production.

Mellgren lives in Stockholm with his wife and two kids. His youngest child, who was three years old when this book was first published, claims that he will soon grow to be as big as a mountain. When this happens, his father will become very little so that the son can carry him around. The author looks forward to this.

Elsa and the Night
by Jöns Mellgren

Translation from Swedish by Anita Shenoi
Proofreading by Kate Brown

Published by Little Gestalten, Berlin 2014

ISBN: 978-3-89955-716-9

Typefaces: Chaparral Pro by Carol Twombly, Neutraface Condensed by Christian Schwartz
Printed by Livonia Print, Riga
Made in Europe

The Swedish original edition *Sigrid och Natten* was published by Natur & Kultur, Stockholm.
© for the Swedish original: Jöns Mellgren and Natur & Kultur, Stockholm 2013
© for the English edition: Little Gestalten, an imprint of Die Gestalten Verlag GmbH & Co. KG, Berlin 2014

For more information, please visit www.gestalten.com.

Bibliographic information published by the Deutsche Nationalbibliothek.
The Deutsche Nationalbibliothek lists this publication in the Deutsche Nationalbibliografie; detailed bibliographic data are available online at http://dnb.d-nb.de.

This book was printed on paper certified by the FSC®.

Gestalten is a climate-neutral company. We collaborate with the non-profit carbon offset provider myclimate (www.myclimate.org) to neutralize the company's carbon footprint produced through our worldwide business activities by investing in projects that reduce CO_2 emissions (www.gestalten.com/myclimate).